Littlenose

More adventures of

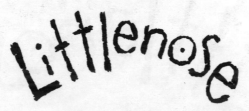

Littlenose
the Magician

JOHN GRANT
Illustrations by Ross Collins

SIMON AND SCHUSTER

SIMON AND SCHUSTER
Littlenose the Magician was first published in 1975
The Old Man's Spear was first published in 1977
The other stories were first published in 1986
in Great Britain by The British Broadcasting Corporation

This collection published by Simon and Schuster UK Ltd, 2009
A CBS COMPANY

1 3 5 7 9 10 8 6 4 2

Simon & Schuster UK Ltd
1st Floor
222 Grays Inn Road
London WC1X 8HB

A CIP catalogue record for this book is available from the British Library

ISBN: 978-1-84738-201-6

Printed and bound in Great Britain by CPI Cox & Wyman, Reading, Berkshire

Contents

Littlenose the Magician

In the days when Littlenose lived, the most important person in the tribe was the Old Man. But, only a little less important was the Doctor. He looked after the sick, as you might expect, but he had other important duties as well.

For instance, he foretold the future. This he did by watching pictures in the fire, or by observing the flight of birds.

But his favourite method was to take out a pack of white birch bark squares with strange markings on them. He spread them out on a flat rock, then turned them up one at a time, muttering as he did so. The people would crowd round his cave saying: "He is going to make a prediction." Then a meeting would be called later in the day at which the Doctor would raise his arms and pronounce in a solemn voice something like: "There is going to be a hard winter!" And considering this was the Ice Age, he had never been wrong!

Littlenose didn't think much of either the Doctor's nasty-tasting medicines or his fortunetelling, but he was filled with awe at the Doctor's other job, that of Tribal Magician. He had only the vaguest idea what magic was, and he had never seen the

Doctor actually perform any, but he heard
a lot about it. He knew, for instance, that
he could make a coloured pebble vanish
and produce it from someone's ear; he had
heard that, with the right magic words,
a handful of old bones could become a
bouquet of flowers; and there was the story
of a rabbit which the doctor had produced
from an empty fur hood.

Someone had once asked why he didn't use his magic to help in useful things like hunting and rain-making as the Straight-noses did. The Doctor was horrified. "It's not for us to meddle with the powers of darkness," he said warningly. "Look what it's done for the Straightnoses. You wouldn't want to end up like them, would you?" And as that was the last thing anyone wanted, it was never mentioned again.

There had been a lot of talk lately about the Doctor and magic, but Littlenose was more concerned with the preparations for the Sun Dance. This was the great mid-winter festival, like a huge party, with singing and dancing and feasting. Presents were given, and everyone had a marvellous time far into the night, even past bed-time for grownups. This year there was to be an

4

extra treat. Occasionally, the Doctor had been persuaded to give a demonstration of magic as part of the entertainment. His last appearance had been before Littlenose was old enough to attend the Sun Dance. In the few days left, the Doctor was very busy, and was quite huffy if anyone arrived at his cave with a sore stomach or toothache. All they got were some dried herbs or a quick drink of something discouraging from the Doctor's wife.

She was his assistant and nurse, and she spent most of her time out of sight at home. Littlenose thought that she was probably ashamed of being so ugly. She was tall and skinny, by Neanderthal standards, with a nose not much bigger than Littlenose's own. She might have been called Littlenose too, but her hair was long, straight and yellow, so she was called Goldie.

It was rumoured that she came from a distant tribe and it was she who had taught the Doctor all he knew.

The Sun Dance came at last and, as usual, it was even better than Littlenose remembered. When they had danced and sung themselves hoarse, and even Littlenose had eaten himself to a standstill, the Old Man stepped forward and announced: "And now, for your delight and delectation, a fabulous feast of mystery and merriment proudly presented by the great. . .DOCTOR!"

The doctor swept into the circle with a flourish. He wore a cloak of some smooth, black fur, and a hood over his head. The hood covered his face so that his eyes shone out from a pair of holes. He looked

mysterious and rather frightening. As the
applause began to die away, the Old Man
threw out an arm and shouted, "Assisted by
the glamorous Goldie!"

The glamorous Goldie ran on to even louder applause. She wore two rabbit ears in her hair, while the rest consisted of all that was left of the rabbit . . . including the tail.

The magic show was everything Littlenose expected and more. Coloured pebbles appeared and reappeared. Old bones became bunches of flowers and, not one but two rabbits were pulled mysteriously from a fur hood. The audience cheered and clapped while Littlenose's eyes grew wider and wider at the wonder of it all. Then the Doctor and the glamorous Goldie carried forward what looked like the trunk of a tree. But as they set it up in front of the audience, Littlenose saw that the log had been hollowed out so that it was really only a

shell of very thin wood and bark. As it was
laid on the ground, he could also see that
it had been split down the centre with the
top half forming a sort of lid.

The Doctor held up his hand for
silence. "I shall now attempt, with the
assistance of the glamorous Goldie, one of
the most hazardous feats of magic known. I
must ask for complete silence. Thank you."

With a flourish, he lifted the lid of the
hollow log and held the glamorous Goldie
by the hand while she climbed inside. She
smiled prettily, waved, and lay down so that
her head stuck out at one end and her feet
at the other. The Doctor stooped down and
picked up the biggest axe Littlenose had
ever seen. The audience gasped as the
Doctor swung it up without effort, and
held their breath as he stood in the circle

of torchlight, which sparkled along the axe's sharp edge. Then, with a crash, the axe hurtled down on to the tree trunk and the glamorous Goldie!

Splinters flew in all directions as the blade buried itself in the ground. People screamed. Some fainted. Littlenose felt sick. But the Doctor was not finished yet. He quickly removed the axe and pulled the two halves of the log apart. There was a clear gap where the glamorous Goldie's middle should have been. Which wasn't surprising . . . and hardly magic!

What was surprising, and could only be magic, was her nodding head and smiling face sticking out of one half, and her wriggling toes sticking out of the other. The audience was again silent as the Doctor quickly pushed the halves together. He waved

his arm, shouted a magic word and raised the lid. The glamorous Goldie stood up and waved. There wasn't a mark on her. She bowed to the audience, and Littlenose expected her top half to fall off. But it didn't, and the Doctor and the glamorous Goldie went off to thunderous applause.

In the weeks following the Sun Dance, Littlenose could think of nothing else but magic. He even tried some, but without success. Things just refused to disappear, and Dad almost split his sides laughing as Littlenose frantically waved an old bone in the air, trying to turn it into a bunch of flowers. "Come on, Littlenose," he said, "you must do better than that. How about cutting a lady in half? I'm sure Mum would help. That is, if you could get her inside a hollow log. Ha! Ha! Ha!" Mum said, "That's not funny."

"Just you wait," said Littlenose. "When I've learned to do a piece of magic, you'll get the biggest surprise of your lives!"

After a few days, Littlenose decided that his magic was getting nowhere. But he had an idea. He would find out how the Doctor did his. He couldn't very well ask him straight out, but if he could creep close enough to his cave, he might see him at work. It was risky. He had once heard the story of a boy who had tried just this and had been turned into a frog!

Next morning, Littlenose set off for the Doctor's cave. As he approached, he could hear voices from inside. He tip-toed to the entrance. The Doctor and his wife were seated with their backs to him, busy at some task . . . probably more magic. Littlenose edged closer but, whatever their task was, they were keeping it well hidden from intruders. He was about to leave, when something caught his attention.

Lying on a rocky ledge just inside the cave entrance was a stick, thick as a finger and about half the length of Littlenose's arm.

It was stained with strange patterns and Littlenose remembered that he had last seen it at the Sun Dance, when the Doctor had used it to wave or point at things he wanted to change into something else or to disappear. In a moment, Littlenose had made up his mind. He would borrow the stick. He wouldn't ask for the loan of it. Just borrow it. In a flash the stick was under his hunting robe. Then Littlenose hurried home as fast as he could.

Slipping to the back of the cave, he tried out the magic stick. He waved it, tapped it and shook it, but nothing disappeared. And nothing changed into anything else. But Littlenose wasn't downhearted. "Practice," he said to himself. "That's what I need." But before he could get any practice, he heard Dad calling him.

"A herd of bison has been seen nearby,"
said Dad, "and we're going out with a party
to hunt them. Get your things. We're
leaving immediately."

Littlenose put on his hunting robe and
picked up his boy-size spear. He wondered
about the magic stick for a moment, then
decided to bind it along the shaft of the
spear. This made it easy to carry and was
unlikely to be noticed.

The hunters had barely left the caves before they realised that something odd was happening. The air was strangely mild and there was a slight thaw, very unusual for this time of year. They trudged on through the wood, Littlenose and Two-Eyes bringing up the rear of the column. They stopped to rest for a moment and Littlenose whispered to Two-Eyes, "Look, there's a robin," and pointed up into a tree. And at that second a great lump of melting snow slid from the tree and fell on one of the hunters with a thump. The man struggled to his feet and shook his fist at Littlenose. "That you up to your tricks?" he shouted. "Throwing things?"

"I didn't throw anything," said Littlenose. "I just pointed. Like that." He did it just as a pine branch, weakened by the weight of snow it was carrying, snapped with a loud crack and tumbled to the ground. The hunters all looked at Littlenose. They looked at the spear he was still pointing. He looked at the stick tied to the spear and began to wonder. However, after a bit of muttering among themselves, the hunters went on their way, but kept a watchful eye on Littlenose.

At length, they reached a small valley with a frozen stream at the bottom. Nosey, the chief stalker, was warily inching his way across but he didn't feel at all safe. Littlenose stood with Two-Eyes some way back from the stream and watched. "I think you're too heavy to cross there, Two-Eyes," he said, and pointed with his spear. There was a loud crack, then a wild yell from Nosey as the ice broke under him and he

vanished into the freezing water.
Littlenose dropped the spear as if it were
red hot.

While the hunters hauled a shivering
Nosey on to the bank, Littlenose untied
the stick and wondered what to do with it.
He had a feeling that just throwing it away
would be no good. He should never have
taken it without asking. He tucked it out of
sight in his furs and planned to give it back
to its rightful owner just as soon as he

reached home. And it looked as if that would be sooner than he'd expected. The bison had gone, leaving no trace, and Nosey was sneezing and shivering from his ducking.

The hunters decided to stop for the night and made a rough shelter out of tree branches and hunting robes. The air had turned heavy and clammy, while inky, black clouds began to pile up in the sky. They had a cold supper and, while there was still some light left, Littlenose wandered off for a stroll before turning in. He carried the magic stick under his robe and had decided to try once more to make it work for him. After all, the disasters of earlier in the day could have been chance. Perhaps.

When he was out of sight of the camp, he picked up a handful of twigs and waved the stick over them. They were meant to turn into a bunch of flowers. Nothing happened, except that a large spot of rain fell on his nose. And that wasn't magic. He tried it on pebbles but they remained obstinately unchanged. He even tapped himself on the head, and was relieved that he didn't turn into a frog. He gave up. The rain was beginning to fall heavily now and the snow grew wet and mushy under his feet.

Littlenose shouted angrily at the stick and shook it hard. "Call yourself magic? You're just an old bit of firewood. I dare you to do something magic!"

There was a blinding flash and a deafening bang. A solitary pine tree high on the hill in front of him was split from top to bottom by a jagged bolt of lightning.

Littlenose fell to the ground in terror and watched the smouldering remains of the tree, as the rain poured down about him and the thunder crashed and boomed about the sky.

Littlenose lay awake all night, quaking with terror. Dad and the other hunters were not sympathetic. "Fancy a big boy like you afraid of thunder," they laughed.

As soon as the hunting party reached home, Littlenose lost no time in returning the stick. He tried to sneak it back the way he had got it but, just as he was creeping up to the cave entrance, a voice said: "What do you think you're playing at?" it was the Doctor.

Littlenose was trapped. "This is it," he thought. "I'll be a frog any minute."

He stood up and held out the stick.

"I was bringing this back. You see, it's like this. I was—"

But the Doctor cut him short. "Oh thanks. Didn't know I'd dropped it. Didn't really matter." And he casually broke the stick into pieces and threw them in the fire.

Littlenose was aghast. The Doctor spoke again. "Here's something for your trouble." And he tossed a coloured pebble at Littlenose. He caught it . . . and it was an apple! "Now, off you go and don't bother me, Sonny. I've got a lot to do."

"Thank you," said Littlenose, thoroughly perplexed. He looked at the apple. Was it magic? He suddenly didn't care about magic any more. He knew he managed to get into enough trouble without the aid of magic.

He started to run towards the cave,
shouting, "Come on, Two-Eyes. I've got an
apple. You can have half."

The Old Man's Spear

The Old Man was leader of the tribe
because he was not only the oldest
member but the wisest. No one knew how
old he was, and they had even less idea of
the extent of his wisdom. As a young man
he had been handsome, strong, swift,
and a famous hunter. But now he was bald,
fat and a bit short of wind. It was years
since he last hunted but he didn't need to,

as he was given a share of all the tribe's food. The Old Man's job was to organise everyone else; and he did it very well.

Yet one spring day when the sun shone, the trees were beginning to turn green and the snow had vanished, the Old Man summoned the hunters to a meeting.

Dad and Littlenose (he was an apprentice hunter), hurried along wondering what calamity was about to strike this time. For the Old Man's meetings usually spelled trouble. When they were all assembled, the Old Man climbed onto a boulder and addressed them. "I intend," he said, "to go hunting. I want you to arrange everything. Make it a week today. Any questions? No? That's it, then. Thank you." And he turned away into his cave.

The hunters were astonished and there was a lot of muttering as the meeting broke up. "Hunting! At his age! He's daft!"

Dad said much the same thing. "You can't say things like that," said Mum, aghast. "He is, after all, the Leader!"

Littlenose saw nothing odd in the Old Man's wanting a bit of fun. He thought it must be very dull with nothing to do all day but make speeches, study the Time Sticks, and tell people what to do. And although Dad and the rest of the grown-up hunters still thought the whole idea ridiculous, the other members of the tribe began to think like Littlenose. They got more and more enthusiastic until, instead of the hunters planning an official hunt for the Old Man, it had become a grand day out and picnic for the whole tribe. Of course, there would still be some hunting, because that, after all, was what the Old Man wanted.

The day of the Old Man's hunt came at last. And there had never been a hunt like it. The hunters hoped that there would never be one like it again. The hunting party, if that's what you could call it, assembled in front of the caves soon after breakfast. Everyone was there. Men, women, children, old people bobbling along on sticks and babies in arms. Dad, Nosey and other men shouted themselves hoarse trying to get some sort of order, while babies cried and older children chased one another through the crowd. When the Old Man at last appeared everyone cheered. He carried a spear that looked even older than himself. "Well, what are we waiting for?" he said. "Let's go."

An ordinary hunting party would consist

of no more than a dozen men, carrying spears and a few pieces of gear for camping out. They would march in a straight line behind the tracker and be absolutely silent, for fear that they would scare away the animals they were hunting. But this was a whole tribe! They carried babies and baskets of food. And they straggled in an untidy crowd behind the Old Man, shouting and laughing at the tops of their voices so that every self-respecting animal fled as fast as its legs would carry it. The hunters found the whole spectacle quite embarrassing, and were glad that no other tribe was around to see it.

Before noon, they stopped in a large clearing and soon a magnificent picnic was under way. The Neanderthal folk ate and drank with gusto, wishing the Old Man "Good Health" and "Long Life and Happiness". After the feast, no one was really disposed to do much in the way of hunting. Not just yet, anyway. And, although the hunters fumed and fretted, the other grown-ups, including the Old Man, settled down for an after-dinner nap, while the children paddled in the stream and tried to catch minnows.

Late in the afternoon, the Old Man stretched and stood up. "I feel twenty years younger," he said. "How about this hunting, then? Have you found something for me to hunt? I think I could manage a sabre-toothed tiger or at least a deer."

The hunters looked at each other and made polite noises, none of them liking to tell the Old Man that

there was unlikely to be anything
bigger than a beetle stirring for miles.
Luckily, the Old Man wasn't really
expecting an answer. He waved his spear
to the crowd, who got to their feet and
followed him with a loud cheer back into
the forest. He was thoroughly enjoying
himself now. He held his spear at the
ready and occasionally held up his hand
for the people to stop. Then he put his
finger to his lips and said, "Sh!" and
everyone else copied him. Then on they
went, scanning the surrounding trees for
anything that might move. Then suddenly
the Old Man cried, "Look!"

No one could say exactly what it was
that the Old Man saw but already his
spear was flying through the air, up
through the branches and leaves

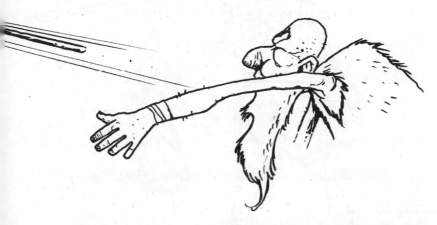

overhead. "Missed by a hair's breadth, Sir!"
cried someone, although what it had been
was still uncertain. What was certain, and
without a shadow of doubt, was that the
spear had not returned to earth. "It was an
eagle. It's flown off with it!" cried another
voice. But Littlenose, who had wriggled to
the front, shouted, "No, it's stuck in a tree.
High up."

"Do you think you could get it down,
my boy?" asked the Old Man.

"I'll try," said Littlenose, and he

attempted to scramble up the trunk. But,
the bark was smooth and slippery, and the
spear could be seen, sticking out high
above the nearest branch. Littlenose came
back shaking his head. Several more
attempts were made but to no avail.

"We might as well leave it," said a hunter.

"It's time to go home and, anyway, it
was just an old spear."

"What do you mean, *old*!" exclaimed

the Old Man. "That spear is an heirloom! It was my father's, and his father's before that. I'll give a reward of five green pebbles to whoever can rescue my spear." There and then Littlenose made up his mind that the reward would be his. All the way home, he plotted and planned but, by the time they reached home, he still had no ideas. In fact, it was as he was dropping off to sleep that the first glimmerings of an idea came into his mind.

In the morning, Littlenose immediately remembered his idea for winning the Old Man's reward. He lay and thought a bit more, then Mum called that breakfast was ready, and he got up. Breakfast was almost over when Littlenose said, "I'm going to learn to fly."

Dad started to laugh. "What was that?

Fly?" he spluttered.

"Yes," said Littlenose. "Then I can get back the Old Man's spear for him."

At this, Dad fell off his seat and rolled on the floor, clutching his sides. "Oh-ho!" he cried. "Wait till I tell everyone. My son! Flying!"

Soon, every member of the tribe had heard of Littlenose's plan, and they laughed as much as Dad. It became a special joke, when someone met Littlenose, to flap their arms like wings and wink at him, so Littlenose quickly resolved to carry out his preparations well away from inquisitive eyes. In any case, people very soon got tired of the joke, except Dad. And he very soon was regarded as a bit of a bore on the subject of flying boys, flapping his arms and winking at everyone he met.

For his experiments in flying, Littlenose chose the part of the forest where the spear had been lost. It wasn't very convenient but he reasoned that, as soon as he had mastered the art of flying, he would want to waste as little time as possible. He started off by watching the birds. They just flapped their wings. And wings were really just sort of arms. So, Littlenose flapped his arms.

He flapped them standing still.
And he flapped them running up and
down. Nothing happened. His shoulders
ached and he was out of breath but he
stayed firmly on the ground. He watched
some more birds. Of course, it must be the
feathers that made the difference! He must
get some.

For once, luck seemed to be going his
way. There was roast goose for supper that
night and the ground outside the cave was
covered with feathers. Littlenose gathered
two large handfuls of the biggest feathers
he could find and hid them in his own
special corner of the cave.

Next day started very early as Dad was
going off for a day's hunting with some
other men. It was barely daylight as
Littlenose watched them making their way

into the forest and, not long after, he too set off, clutching the goose feathers.

Littlenose was almost at the clearing when he heard voices. Carefully, he crept through the trees until he could see a group of figures. It was the hunting party! But they were not hunting. Far from it. They were sorting out a complicated system of rawhide ropes and talked as they worked.

"Do you honestly think that this is going to be any good?" asked one man.

"As good as anything anybody else has tried," replied another.

Dad spoke. "Nosey, here, had a good plan. He was just going to cut the tree down with his stone axe. But the Old Man wouldn't let him. Something about the tree falling on the spear and breaking it. Mind you, my boy Littlenose had the best plan.

He said he would fly up and get the spear."
He flapped his arms and laughed loudly,
although no one else did.

Littlenose was furious. The men weren't
hunting - they were after the reward! There
was no point in trying while they were all
messing around with ropes and things.
Angry and disappointed, Littlenose threw

the goose feathers away and went home. It seemed certain that the grown-ups would rescue the spear and earn the five green pebbles.

But things didn't quite turn out that way. Dad arrived home in the evening, and Mum said, "Had a good day in the forest, dear?" Dad said, "Hmph! Not a thing." And Littlenose's spirits rose. Whatever their scheme, the hunters must have failed; which served them right for being deceitful.

Then Mum said, "I hear the Doctor is planning to use magic to bring the Old Man's spear down from the tree."

Dad gave a short laugh. "Hah!" he exclaimed. "The Doctor can't even do the three pebble trick properly!"

Littlenose felt a little more optimistic,

and he began to think again. When people like Dad failed in something, they usually gave up. All that he had to do was wait for the winter gales, when the spear was certain to be blown down. He must make sure to be first there to pick it up.

So spring passed into summer and then came autumn. Littlenose visited the clearing from time to time, and still the spear remained where it was. In this particular clearing many of the trees bore fruit or nuts, and one autumn day Littlenose went off with Two-Eyes to pick some. There was a good crop, but one particular nut tree was loaded. There was only one problem. The nuts were high up, and the tree was so slender that when Littlenose tried to climb it, it bent and shook alarmingly. Next day, he went

back, this time equipped with Mum's
rawhide clothes line, which she didn't
happen to be using just at that moment
and wouldn't miss. He climbed as high as
he could and tied one end of the rope
firmly to the slender trunk. Then he
scrambled down and gave the other end
to Two-Eyes. Two-Eyes was small but
strong and together they hauled on the
rope until the tree bent down a little.
Then they hauled some more. And again.

It took most of the day but, eventually,
Littlenose and Two-Eyes sat back
exhausted and admired the result of their
efforts. The slender nut tree was now bent
right down so that the topmost twigs
touched the ground. The rope was tied to
a handy tree stump, and they could
gather all the nuts they wanted without

leaving the ground. But before they could
gather a single nut, there came an irate
shout. "Littlenose! What are you playing
at? No wonder there's no game. You've
scared everything away. Clear off!
Go home!"

It was Dad, followed by a hunting party.
Dad came towards Littlenose, paying no
attention to the tied-down tree, and started
to climb over it. Now, Littlenose's knots
were not very good at the best of times,

and Dad was half-way over when the knot
fastening the rope to the tree stump gave
way. There was a swish, a rustle, and a yell.
The tree sprang back straight again. And
Dad vanished. The hunters looked up in
time to see Dad sailing gracefully into the
tree-tops. He grabbed at a branch to save
himself, but it came away in his hand and
he came to earth in a briar thicket. There
the others found him, scratched, bruised
and dazed, and holding in his hand, not a
branch . . . but the Old Man's spear!

Poor Dad! All the way home and for
weeks after, everyone greeted him with
flapping arms and a broad wink. They
called him Birdman behind his back.
Littlenose thought they were very unkind.
At least, the Old Man had his precious
spear back! However, he declared that,

45

since no one person had rescued it, the
reward should go towards the cost of
another tribal outing in the summer. So
everyone was happy. Except, perhaps,
Littlenose, until one day the Old Man
called him aside and gave him a special
reward of a white pebble for himself.
Which made up slightly for what happened
when Mum discovered the state of her
clothes line!

Littlenose and Two-Eyes

Littlenose sat under his favourite tree.
Two-Eyes was sitting beside him and, for
once, Littlenose paid no attention to the
little mammoth. Even when Two-Eyes
gave a squeak and prodded Littlenose
with his trunk, Littlenose brushed it aside
and said, "Don't bother me, Two-Eyes.
I'm busy, can't you see?"

Two-Eyes couldn't see, and he got

to his feet and went off in a huff.

Littlenose settled back against the tree, closed his eyes, and began mumbling to himself. He was learning a poem. It had all started a week ago. To everyone's surprise, not least of all Littlenose's, he had passed each of his tests for promotion from apprentice to junior hunter. Actually, he had one more test to do, which was the reason for the poem. He had passed fire-lighting with distinction, tracking with top marks, and spear throwing . . . just! But now he had the last and final test. It was called Hunting the Grey Bear.

There wasn't really a grey bear, or any other colour of bear for that matter. Three pieces of wood were tied together in a special way and covered with grey fur.

This was carefully hidden, and the apprentice hunter had to find it by following clues.

The clues formed a poem and it was this that Littlenose was memorising. It didn't seem to make a lot of sense, which didn't make it any easier to learn:

The Grey Bear's prints are in the clay,
The noon-day shadow points the way,
The island's where the heron cries,
The ashwood close on willow lies,
The peak where pine grows to the sky,
The Grey Bear in his den does lie!

Littlenose said it once through to himself, then once more out loud. As long as he remembered it tomorrow, all he had to do was work out what it all meant.

Next morning, Littlenose was up before it was light. After a quick breakfast, he hurried to the Old Man's cave carrying his boy-size spear. There was quite a crowd of hunters waiting to see him off. Dad wasn't there. He had gone off even earlier with another man to hide the Grey Bear. The Old Man made a short speech about how he hoped that Littlenose's name would be inscribed on the birch-bark roll of junior hunters. Then he gave Littlenose a tightly-wrapped package, food for the day "not to be eaten until the third line of the poem".

Littlenose took the package, said thank you, and set off while everyone shouted: "Good luck!"

As he left the caves behind, he was
quite sure of the first clue. The only clay
around was close to the river and was used
by the Neanderthal folk for making pots
and bowls. Sure enough, there was a line
of marks in the clay that looked more or
less like bear prints. As he looked, there
was a noise, and out from among the trees
trotted Two-Eyes.

"Go home," shouted Littlenose. "You can't come. This is all very important."

The little mammoth looked very crestfallen, and Littlenose turned his back and began to hurry along the line of tracks. The tracks left the clay but Littlenose found them easily as they crossed grassy patches, led through the pinewoods and took him far across a sandy heath.

Then they stopped. Just like that!

What was the next line of the poem?

The noon-day shadow points the way.

What shadow? Which way? It was almost noon now. He stood, perplexed. Then there was a quiet snuffle behind him. He jumped round.

"Two-Eyes!" he shouted. "What do you mean, following me like that? This is work for hunters, not mammoths!"

He started to think again about noon-day shadows, when Two-Eyes squeaked once more. He was standing pointing with his trunk to something on the ground. Right where the bear tracks ended was a rock. "That's no good," said Littlenose. "It's too sunken in the grass to cast a shadow." Two-Eyes pointed again with his trunk. The rock was chipped and cracked, and in the centre was a hole slightly bigger than a finger. "Of course," cried Littlenose. "You are a clever mammoth!"

He took his spear and stuck it upright in the hole in the rock. It was noon. The shadow of the spear lay along the grass, and at its tip was a white stone. A few steps away was another, then another. If he went from stone to stone

he should come to: *The island's where the heron cries*. He hoped it wasn't too far. He couldn't open his packed lunch till then, and he was getting hungry.

The white stones led in a wandering way over open country. Ahead, Littlenose could see low trees and bushes and the glint of water. As he got nearer, the ground underfoot grew damp. There were stagnant pools and clumps of reeds. He came to the end of the trail of white stones and found himself on the edge of a wide marsh. A broad, slow-flowing river lay across his path.

Littlenose and Two-Eyes splashed the short distance to the river. There were willow trees along the bank, and others growing on a couple of islands. Which was the island with the herons, he wondered? Two-Eyes nudged him with his trunk. Littlenose turned. A heron was pacing majestically through the shallows by the bank. It stood still for several moments, peering down into the water. Then   , quick as a flash, its long beak darted into the water and came up with a wriggling fish. Littlenose watched. The heron slipped

the fish into its crop, then rose into the air
on enormous wings. It circled round and
dropped down into the top of a tree on the
farthest-away island. "That's it," said
Littlenose. "That's the one!"

Followed by a reluctant mammoth –
Two-Eyes didn't like getting his fur wet –
Littlenose waded into the river. The water

was little more than knee deep, and they quickly reached the island. There were several heron nests in the trees, and the big birds screeched at the intruders.

"Well, the herons are crying, all right," said Littlenose. "That's the third line of the poem. Now I can eat my lunch." He opened the tightly-wrapped skin package. The Old Man had given him several pieces of prime venison. But . . . it was raw! It must be part of the test. All he had to do was build a fire.

It came as a nasty shock to find that there seemed to be nothing to build a fire *with*! The island was low-lying and swampy, and the few twigs and sticks Littlenose found lying in the grass were too wet to burn. Again, it was Two-Eyes who came to the rescue. He went over to one of the trees and reached up with his trunk. The branches were loaded with dead grass and sticks brought down in the winter floods, all perfectly dry. Littlenose stood on Two-Eyes' back and dragged down an armful. Quickly, he struck a light with his flints and, in a short time, the venison was toasting over the flames.

Fed and contented, Littlenose sat on a low willow branch and thought, while Two-Eyes grazed nearby. That was half the clues used up, although he had to admit that without Two-Eyes' help, he wouldn't have done so well! Why, if he weren't a mammoth, he might make a pretty good hunter himself. What was the next part of the poem?

The ashwood close on willow lies.

That wasn't much help. There was

plenty of willow. In fact, there was nothing else. Where did the bit about "ash" fit in? Was it perhaps among the driftwood in the trees? Oh dear! What if he'd burnt it in his cooking fire! He jumped down and picked up his spear. And as he did so, he remembered, the Neanderthal Folk used ash for spear and axe handles. It must mean his spear. Another thought struck him, and he climbed back on the willow branch. Yes! He'd wondered about the fresh marks cut in the bark. They were made just where small branches formed forks. He took the spear and rested it in the forks. It fitted perfectly, as if they were made for it . . . which they probably were! And the spear pointed straight back across the river towards a distant hill. That's where he had to go now.

The hill was farther away than
Littlenose first thought and it was late
afternoon before he came near its foot. It
was really a small mountain. The lower
slopes were quite bare – they seemed to
consist of red gravel. Higher up was red
rock. The rock formed weird peaks and
pinnacles.

The peak where pine grows to the sky,
The Grey Bear in his den does lie!

And there, just visible against the sky, was
the twisted shape of an ancient pine
clinging to the summit of one of the
pinnacles. There was the end of the trail.
Somewhere up there were three pieces of
wood tied together in a strange fashion and
covered with grey fur. All he had to do was

climb up and get it.

Littlenose strained his eyes to find an easy route to the summit. He paused. He could see people. Two figures seemed to be hiding behind one of the smaller pinnacles lower down. Of course! That would be Dad and his friend who had hidden the Grey Bear. He would pretend he hadn't seen them.

Littlenose and Two-Eyes circled round the base of the hill. And to their delight, they found that a path led almost to the top. Up they went, arriving panting close under the pine tree. It grew out of a crack above Littlenose's head, but the rock seemed quite impossible to climb. They stood precariously at the top of the gravel slope and wondered where on earth the Grey Bear could be hidden.

While Littlenose poked about, Two-Eyes

had been looking down to the foot. He
gave a sudden soft squeak. "What is it?"
said Littlenose. "Have you found it?"

He followed Two-eyes' gaze . . . and his
heart almost stopped. Half-way up, a huge

black bear stood, rearing up on its hind legs. It had been hidden from below by the rocks. That was why Dad and his friend were hiding! Not from Littlenose. The bear took a couple of steps, but the gravel slipped under its feet. It couldn't get at the hunters, but it was prepared to wait!

"We must do something, Two-Eyes," said Littlenose. And he pulled himself up on to part of the rock for a better view. Too late, he realised that the rock was loose. He flung himself to one side as the rock crashed down the hill. He fell against Two-eyes and together they rolled down after the rock in a great cloud of red dust.

The bear leapt back in fright. What was this? A landslide . . . and a cloud of dust that made a noise like an angry mammoth! To crown it all, a large rock bounced out from the dust cloud just missing the bear's head. Without a backward glance, it turned and fled.

As the dust cleared, Dad and the other man ran to join Littlenose and Two-eyes. "That was one of the bravest things I've ever seen," said Dad. "And, of course, congratulations!"

Littlenose looked down. Brought down with the stones and gravel, and lying at his feet, was the Grey Bear.

That night, Littlenose stood proudly as the Old Man took a piece of charcoal and made the marks on the roll of junior hunters that meant 'Littlenose'. Dad whispered something in the Old Man's ear. The Old Man smiled and added: "and Two-Eyes".

"You two really are a team," he said.

"I knew Two-Eyes would make a
hunter," thought Littlenose. Then he
hurried home, hoping that being a junior
hunter meant that he was now allowed to
stay up late with the grown-ups.

The Amber Pendant

Next to the Old Man, who was Chief,
the most important person in Littlenose's
tribe was the Doctor. And this was not
only because he cured people when they
were sick, but because he was also a
magician! Everyone was a bit afraid of
the Doctor. Some said that he wasn't
Neanderthal at all. That was why he
never appeared without the ceremonial

mask which hid his face. Some even went as far as to say the he was really a Straightnose – which explained why he was so clever.

The Doctor's wife, Goldie, was even more of a mystery. By Neanderthal standards she was almost unbelievably ugly. Her hair was long and golden and her nose was not much bigger than Littlenose's. She rarely ventured from her cave, and people said that the Doctor was ashamed of her. Of course, they didn't say that to his face. You don't go around talking about someone whose husband could easily turn you into a frog or worse.

One evening, Dad came home and said, "The Doctor's wife has lost an amber pendant. He's offering a reward to whoever finds it."

Littlenose looked up from his supper. "I bet I find it," he said. "What's a pendant?"

"She wears it around her neck," said Dad. "Two pieces of amber on a leather thong."

"I see," said Littlenose. "And what's amber?"

Dad sighed. He thought for a moment. "It's yellow stuff. With flies in it. And it's magic."

Littlenose tried to picture it for himself. Yellow? Flies? All he could think about was egg yolk – with greedy flies getting their legs stuck. And magic? Magic egg yolk? He tried to imagine the Doctor's wife wearing two runny eggs covered with flies. Grown-ups were even odder people than he thought! But the reward! He didn't care

what he found as long as he got the
reward.

First thing after breakfast next day, he
set off with Two-Eyes to hunt for the
missing amber pendant. And it was a lot
more difficult than he had imagined.
Littlenose thought that all he had to do
was keep his eyes open for something
yellow. He said so to Two-Eyes. "Then we

check it for the flies," he said.

Two-Eyes sighed. Life with Littlenose was never dull, but it was sometimes hard for a young mammoth to understand what was going on.

They walked along by the river. People often lost things while they were fishing or just out walking, thought Littlenose. He peered at the ground and at the shallow water near the bank. Then he stopped. "Look, Two-Eyes!" he cried. Something bright and yellow shone among the small waves. He jumped down the bank. And saw that it was only the sunlight shining on the pebbles. Ah, well! Better luck next time!

Then it was Two-Eyes' turn. He gave a squeak and pointed with his trunk. In the shadow of a tree were two, bright yellow objects. Littlenose rushed to pick them up.

But before he had got half-way the two objects rose into the air and fluttered away among the trees. "Butterflies!" cried Littlenose. "You really are stupid, Two-Eyes!"

"He's a fine one to talk," muttered Two-Eyes in mammoth language, as they went on their way.

They came out of the trees into a wide clearing on the far side of which was a high outcrop of rock. And in the face of the rock was what looked like the opening of a cave. It looked promising as a place to find lost property. In any case, Littlenose liked exploring, despite the number of times he had been warned about going into strange caves.

Littlenose walked boldly into the dark entrance but Two-Eyes hung back. His mammoth senses told him that all was not well. Reluctantly, with a bit of persuasion, he followed Littlenose. And Littlenose had only taken a few steps when he stopped. At the back of the cave were two brightly-shining yellow objects. Littlenose could hardly believe his luck! It couldn't be the sun shining this time. And butterflies didn't live in caves. Then he paused. One of the yellow objects had disappeared for a moment. Almost as if it had blinked. "I

must have imagined it," thought Littlenose.
"This is certainly my lucky day!"

"This is certainly my lucky day,"
thought the sabre-toothed tiger. It had
been having a quiet nap at the back of the
cave when Littlenose had come charging
in. Here, before its very eyes, was its
favourite mid-morning snack: fresh, tender
Neanderthal boy, walking straight up to it!

So as not to waste a moment,
the sabre-toothed tiger opened
its jaws wide, and waited.
Littlenose jumped as
underneath the two bright
shining objects appeared two
rows of bright shining white teeth.
And as he grew

accustomed to the dim light in the cave, he
made out the shape of a sabre-toothed
tiger! He was too terrified to move, even
when the tiger rose to its feet and began to
purr at the thought of fresh boy. Then it
jumped back, startled. It hadn't seen Two-
Eyes' dark fur among the shadows. But now
the little mammoth trumpeted as loud as

he could. The echoes in the cave made it sound like a whole herd. And when the tiger saw a red eye and a green eye shining out at it, it didn't know what to think. Before it could make up its mind, Littlenose and Two-Eyes were out of the cave and running like the wind. They didn't stop until they were close to the caves where the tribe lived.

They knew the tiger would not pursue them there, so they sat down under a willow tree to recover their breath.

Littlenose put his hand on the ground and felt something in the grass. It was a rabbit's paw . . . but without the rabbit. Someone had taken the trouble to bind it round with strips of leather, and there was a loop as if it were meant to hang on something.

"Strange," thought Littlenose. "Perhaps Uncle Redhead will know what it's for." And he tucked it into the secret pocket in his furs.

But he was no nearer finding the amber pendant. "Come on, Two-Eyes," he said. "It will soon be lunchtime. Let's have one more look."

Littlenose started off, but it was marshy ground and Two-Eyes didn't like to get his

fur wet. He went the long way round.
Suddenly, Littlenose heard him squeal.
The little mammoth was standing, pointing
with his trunk. Littlenose ran to join him.
He couldn't see anything at first, but the
breeze stirred a clump of rushes and he
caught a quick glimpse of something bright
yellow. Again he splashed through the
pools of water. . . and found himself
looking at a clump of marsh marigolds.
The bright yellow blooms nodded in the
wind and made reflections in the water.

This was it, decided Littlenose. Reward or
no reward, he had had enough of lost amber
pendants. It was almost lunchtime. If he
could think of nothing better to do, he would
start looking again in the afternoon . . .
perhaps! Mum liked flowers, though, and it
would be nice to take a bunch back to her.

Littlenose picked a big bouquet of marsh marigolds and set off home.

He was almost there when he realised that he was close to the cave where the Doctor lived with his ugly wife. There was the cave, and someone was moving about outside. It was Goldie. She was preparing her husband's lunch, and sat on a rock in the sunshine plucking a pigeon. Littlenose knew that it was rude to stare, but he went closer and stopped to look at Goldie. She wasn't really all that ugly, even if she did have golden hair instead of the dark Neanderthal variety. And small noses weren't a total disaster, thought Littlenose, touching his own.

Suddenly, Goldie looked up. She smiled. "You're Littlenose, aren't you?" she said.

"Yes," said Littlenose, "and —"

"And you've brought me flowers!" cried Goldie.

"Well, really . . ." began Littlenose. Then he stopped and handed the bunch of marsh marigolds to her. "I've been out all morning looking for your amber pendant," he said. "And I haven't found it."

"I'm not surprised," replied Goldie. "It was never lost. The Doctor had no sooner offered the reward than I found it lying where it had fallen in a dark corner of the cave. I don't suppose he's got round to telling people yet. I'm sorry you were put to so much trouble. Would you like to see it?"

Littlenose nodded, not quite sure. Goldie went into the cave and came out carrying what looked like two large golden

pebbles strung on a leather thong. But they weren't pebbles. Littlenose could see right inside them.

"Take them," said Goldie. "Look at the insects trapped inside." Littlenose drew back. "Don't be afraid," said Goldie.

"What about the magic?" asked Littlenose fearfully.

"Oh that," laughed Goldie. "I'll show you in a moment."

Littlenose took the pendant in his hand

and held it up. True enough, there were several small flies and midges embedded in the amber.

Goldie took the pendant again and rubbed one of the pieces of amber vigorously against her furs. Then she held it over some of the small feathers plucked from the pigeon and, as Littlenose watched, the feathers floated upwards and clung to the amber.

"That's it," said Goldie. "Not very useful magic." Littlenose nodded in agreement. "Well I must get on," said Goldie. "A cavewife's work is never done. Thank you for calling. And for the flowers. Goodbye."

Littlenose was at his own cave when he remembered the rabbit's paw he had found. He must remember to ask Uncle Redhead about it next time

he visited. He took it out of his pocket
and was walking head down examining
it when he bumped into someone.
It was Nosey, the Chief Tracker of the
tribe.

"Can't you watch where you're going?"
he shouted. "You youngsters have no
consideration! In my young day
. . . hi! What's that you've got there?"

"I found it," said Littlenose.

"Clever lad! Clever lad!" shouted
Nosey. "My lucky rabbit's foot! I've been
lost without it! How can I ever repay
you? Here!" And he thrust a handful
of coloured pebbles at Littlenose,
enough to buy all sorts of good things at
the next market.

Littlenose stood deep in thought.
What a strange day it had been! He had

almost been eaten by a sabre-toothed tiger, looking for a pendant that wasn't lost. And now he had a reward for finding a piece of dead rabbit.

"Come on, Two-Eyes," he said. "Let's see what's for lunch."

Rock-a-Bye Littlenose

Night had fallen and, in the caves of the
Neanderthal Folk, everyone was asleep.
Except Littlenose. He tossed and he
turned. He sat up in bed and lay down
again. "For goodness' sake, Littlenose,"
shouted Dad, "go to sleep! You're keeping
everyone awake!"

This wasn't quite true, however, as
Mum was only awake because Dad was

shouting, and Two-Eyes was fast asleep in a corner.

"I can't get to sleep," said Littlenose. "My bed's full of bumps and wrinkles!"

"If you made your bed properly every morning as Mum tells you," said Dad, "this sort of thing wouldn't happen!"

Littlenose lay down and pulled the covers over his head and, surprisingly, was soon fast asleep.

When Littlenose woke next morning, he ached all over. "It's your own fault," said Mum. "You can spend this morning airing and shaking your bed and re-making it properly." A Neanderthal bed was a pile of bear skins and other furs, which served as both mattress and covers and was spread on the floor of the cave.

Littlenose began to drag his bedding out

into the middle of the cave. It was quite
remarkable what came to light, and even
more remarkable that he managed to sleep
at all. There was an old flint knife and
some lucky coloured pebbles in the fold of
one fur. Lifting up another, an apple core
and a couple of old bones tumbled out –
the remains of a midnight snack. At the
very bottom of the heap, a particularly hard

lump was revealed as a spare fire-making
flint. It was exciting! Like a treasure hunt!

"Now," said Mum, get those furs outside and beat them until they are clean." And Littlenose laid out the furs on a rock and beat them vigorously with a long stick. He raised clouds of dust. When Mum was satisfied that the bedding was clean and fresh, Littlenose wearily carried it back into the cave to his own special corner.

Then he called to Two-Eyes and, together, they made their way to Littlenose's favourite tree where they did their more important thinking.

Littlenose said, "You know, Two-Eyes, people are pretty unreasonable. Sleeping on the floor, I mean. It's all right for you. With your fur, you could sleep on a bed of thistles without even noticing." He leaned back and watched a bird

disappear into the foliage above his head.
"Now, birds have more sense," he said.
"No lying on the hard ground for them;
they build nests with wool and feathers
and things to line them. And I bet they
never lose a single wink of sleep.

"Suddenly, he leapt to his
feet and shouted: "I'VE
GOT IT, TWO-EYES!"
Startled, Two-Eyes jumped
sideways and gave Littlenose
a suspicious look.

Littlenose's ideas usually spelt trouble for someone – more often than not for Two-Eyes. He sneaked away as Littlenose paced up and down waving his arms as he explained his great idea.

"People nests!" he said. "If people had nests like the birds, there would be none of this business of hard floors. At bedtime they would simply snuggle down and be lulled to sleep by the gently swaying of the branches." There and then, he decided to build a 'people nest', or rather, a 'boy nest' to prove that it could be done.

From the sun, Littlenose judged that it was almost lunch-time, but there was a lot he could do before then. He had to find a suitable tree, for instance. He set off into the woods.

He was deep in the forest before he

found what he was looking for. A tall
straight tree with plenty of hand and foot-
holds for climbing and, right at the top, a
stout limb growing straight out from the
trunk with a large fork at the end. He
started to gather twigs and branches for his
nest. The time flew past, and Littlenose
forgot completely that he should have been
home for lunch.

Then came the tricky part, getting the
twigs and branches to the top of the tree
and building the nest. Littlenose could
only carry one branch at a time as he
climbed carefully to the fork. Soon his
limbs ached and he was scratched and
sore. The branches seemed to get heavier
and heavier but, in the end, the last one
was up and carefully balanced with the
others across the forked branch.

Then he took his flint knife out of his furs and carefully cut strips of bark about as long as his forearm and as broad as his finger. He began to arrange the nesting material across the fork, using the strips of bark to lash it firmly in place. Slowly the nest began to take shape. It was bowl-shaped and beginning to look very nest-like when he realised that he had run out of twigs. He didn't need many. Just enough leafy ones to make a soft and comfortable lining. He slid back along the branch to the trunk and broke off all the leafy branches he could reach and threw them into the nest. Then he hung down and collected more from lower down. It was a simple matter to arrange them inside the woven branches – and the job was done. Littlenose looked at his handiwork

with pride.
Carefully,
he lay
down on
the soft leaves.
He watched the
clouds drift across the sky.
The nest rocked gently in
the tree-top. And Littlenose
fell asleep!

When Littlenose didn't turn up
at lunchtime, Mum was angry. But
when there was still no sign of him
at suppertime, she became worried.
For Littlenose to miss two meals in
a row was most unusual. Dad came
home and a full-scale search was
mounted. With some reluctance
and a lot of muttering, the search

party assembled in the gathering dusk.

"If that boy were mine," grumbled one man, "I'd throw him to the bears!"

"They'd throw him right back," said another. "Bears have more sense!"

They were just leaving when a strange figure stumbled into the circle of torchlight. It was an old, old man. He carried a bundle of sticks in one shaking hand as he lurched and stumbled into the midst of the search party. He grabbed one man by the arm and wheezed and puffed, trying to speak and get his wind back at the same time.

"It's old Nod," said Dad. "What on earth's the matter with him?" Nod was a simple old man who spent most of his time collecting herbs. He had evidently been gathering firewood in the forest.

After a moment, Nod calmed down a

bit and stopped gasping. Then he pointed
dramatically back the way he had come
and cried, "Big as a mammoth! Out of the
sky! It'll have us all!"

"What will?" asked Dad.

"IT!" cried Nod. And he darted about
flapping his arms like wings and talking so

fast that only one word in ten made sense. Then they realised what Nod was telling them. He'd fled for his life from a giant bird! No, he hadn't actually seen a giant bird; but he had seen a giant nest! What more did they want?

"Could you lead us to it?" asked Dad. Nod was perhaps simple but he was not stupid. Bringing word of a ferocious giant bird in the forest was one thing – going back for another look was something else altogether. He gathered up his firewood and hurried off towards his cave.

"Silly old man," said Dad. "Probably imagined the whole thing! Come on. We've wasted enough time as it is." And off they set on their delayed hunt for the missing Littlenose. By the light of their torches, the search party peered into the shadows and

prodded the undergrowth
with their spears, but of
Littlenose there was no
sign. "You don't
suppose the giant bird
got him?" said someone.

"You don't believe that
nonsense, do you?" said Dad,
and he started to laugh. But no-
one else did.

The moon had risen and
Dad realised that the others
were not even looking at him.
They were gazing across a
clearing to where a
tall tree grew slightly
separate from the rest.
Their eyes travelled up
the trunk. Up and up to

97

where a large branch grew out near the top. And there they saw it. There could be no doubt. It was a nest. But what a nest!

"What do we do now?" they asked one another.

Littlenose woke with a start. He hadn't meant to sleep and now it was dark. He climbed out of his nest and slid along the branch to the trunk of the tree. He felt in the light of the moon for foot- and hand-holds. And there were none! Where were all the branches he had used to climb up? Then he remembered. The leafy branches he had broken off to make a comfortable lining were the very branches he had used. He was stuck. He got back into the nest, took a deep breath, and shouted: "HELP!"

To his amazement, there was an immediate reply. A voice out of the darkness shouted, "HI!" Then other voices joined in, including Dad's. They were all talking at once. Mainly nonsense, by the sound. "It's Littlenose! It must have got him! Do you think he's all right? Are you all right, Littlenose?"

"Yes," cried Littlenose. "But I can't get down."

"Hang on!" shouted Dad and, slinging a coil of rawhide rope around his shoulder, he began to climb the tree. He reached the last of the hand-holds, balanced himself as best he could, and tied one end of the rope around his waist. "Tie the end to the branch," he called, throwing the coiled rope to Littlenose. Littlenose did so and waited to see what Dad intended to do next. He never found out because, at that moment, Dad lost his balance and, with a horrible yell, vanished into the darkness. The search party scattered as Dad plummeted towards them. But the rope had got into a great tangle and Dad was brought up short half-way to the ground, dangling helplessly. "Don't all just stand there," he cried. "Get me down!"

"I'll get you down," came Littlenose's voice.

Dad looked up. "No, not THAT!" he cried.

Littlenose was clinging to the branch and sawing at the rawhide rope with his flint knife. "Almost there," he called encouragingly. And before Dad could utter another protest, the rope parted. For the second time, Dad hurtled groundwards. He collided head-on with one of the search party. Luckily, Neanderthal heads were made for rough

treatment. Even as they tumbled in a heap, another body crashed amongst them. Suddenly relieved of Dad's weight, the branch had sprung upwards, catapulting Littlenose into the air. The piled-up search party broke his fall safely, if a bit abruptly.

They got to their feet, picked up the scattered torches and looked at Littlenose. "Look at those scratches," they said. "Must be claw marks. Or beak marks. What an experience!"

Dad said, "We'd better not hang around in case it comes back." And off they hurried with Littlenose, not even scolding him for all the bother he'd caused. It was all very strange. Mum even burst into tears when he got home.

Still bewildered, Littlenose found himself washed, fed and tucked up in bed.

And of one thing he was now certain. Nests were so much trouble that anyone who preferred a nest to a good solid floor must be positively bird-brained!

100,000 YEARS AGO people wore no clothes. They lived in caves and hunted animals for food. They were called NEANDERTHAL.

50,000 YEARS AGO when Littlenose lived, clothes were made out of fur. But now there were other people. Littlenose called them Straightnoses. Their proper name is HOMO SAPIENS.

5,000 YEARS AGO there were no Neanderthal people left. People wore cloth as well as fur. They built in wood and stone. They grew crops and kept cattle.

1,000 YEARS AGO towns were built, and men began to travel far from home by land and sea to explore the world.

500 YEARS AGO towns became larger, as did the ships in which men travelled. The houses they built were very like those we see today.

100 YEARS AGO people used machines to do a lot of the harder work. They could now travel by steam train. Towns and cities became very big, with factories as well as houses.

TODAY we don't hunt for our food, but buy it in shops. We travel by car and aeroplane. Littlenose would not understand any of this. Would YOU like to live as Littlenose did?